Frog Can Hop

written by **LAURA GEHL**   illustrated by **FRED BLUNT**

Ready-to-Read

Simon Spotlight

New York   London   Toronto   Sydney   New Delhi

Here is a list of all the words you will find in this book. Sound them out before you begin reading the story.

Names:

Frog   Pig

SIMON SPOTLIGHT

An imprint of Simon & Schuster Children's Publishing Division
1230 Avenue of the Americas, New York, New York 10020
This Simon Spotlight edition December 2023
Text copyright © 2023 by Laura Gehl
Illustrations copyright © 2023 by Fred Blunt
SIMON SPOTLIGHT, READY-TO-READ, and colophon
are registered trademarks of Simon & Schuster, Inc.
For information about special discounts for bulk purchases, please contact Simon & Schuster
Special Sales at 1-866-506-1949 or business@simonandschuster.com.
Manufactured in the United States of America 1123 LAK
2 4 6 8 10 9 7 5 3 1
Library of Congress Cataloging-in-Publication Data
Names: Gehl, Laura, author. | Blunt, Fred, illustrator. Title: Frog can hop / written by Laura
Gehl ; illustrated by Fred Blunt. Description: Simon Spotlight edition. | New York : Simon
Spotlight, 2023. | Series: Ready-to-read: ready-to-go | Summary: "Frog can hop. Pig likes to
flop. When Frog makes a big drop, will Pig help?"— Provided by publisher. Identifiers: LCCN
2022058223 (print) | LCCN 2022058224 (ebook) | ISBN 9781665920421 (paperback) |
ISBN 9781665920438 (hardcover) | ISBN 9781665920445 (ebook) Subjects: LCSH: Readers
(Primary) | LCGFT: Readers (Publications).
Classification: LCC PE1119.2 .G484 2023 (print) | LCC PE1119.2 (ebook)
DDC 428.6/2—dc23/eng/20230526
LC record available at https://lccn.loc.gov/2022058223
LC ebook record available at https://lccn.loc.gov/2022058224

Word families:

"-op" ⟶ bop   chop

drop   flop

hop   mop

plop   pop

shop   stop

Sight words:

and   can

Ready to go? Happy reading!

Don't miss the questions about the story
on the last page of this book.

Frog can hop.

Pig can flop.

Frog can mop.

Pig can flop.

Frog can shop.

Pig can flop.

Frog can chop.

Pig can flop.

Frog can bop.

Pig can flop.

Frog can . . .

DROP!

Frog can flop.

Pig can mop.

Pig can shop.

Pig can pop.

Pig can bop.

Frog and Pig
can mop.

Frog and Pig
can plop.

Frog and Pig
can hop!

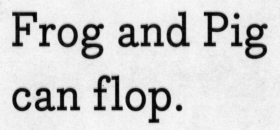

Frog and Pig
can flop.

Now that you have read the story, can you answer these questions?

1. At the beginning of the story, who is shopping?

2. What happens after Frog drops the food?

3. In this story you read the words "bop," "chop," "drop," "flop," "hop," "mop," "plop," "pop," "shop," and "stop." Those words all rhyme! Can you think of another word that rhymes with these words?

Great job!
You are a reading star!